Also by

ROJÉ AUGUSTIN

The Unraveling of Bebe Jones

Rojé Augustin

OUT OF NO WAY

Madam C.J. Walker & A'Lelia Walker

A poetic drama

BOUKMAN

PRESS

BOUKMAN PRESS

First published in 2020 by Boukman Press
Library of Congress Cataloging-in-Publication Data 1-6927063281
Author: Rojé Augustin
Title: Out of No Way, Madam C.J. Walker & A'Lelia Walker A Poetic Drama —
2nd Boukman Press ed.

p. cm. — (Boukman Press)
ISBN 978-0-9873734-7-2

I. Title.

Cover image credit: Madam C.J. Walker Collection, Indian Historical Society
Cover design by Ben Keating

Author's Note:
The poems in this collection are written as if from the subject's point of view. A number of historical figures are referenced in this work as well. However, these poems are a re-telling of historical records about the life of Madam C.J. Walker and her daughter A'Lelia Walker. They are largely inspired by biographies and archival materials. The points of view and themes on which the poems are based are products of the author's imagination and are used fictitiously. Any resemblance to actual events, locales, or persons living or dead is entirely coincidental.

The author has contacted copyright holders for materials used in this book. However, some of the visuals are in the public domain or of unknown origin. Any person or organisation who may have been overlooked should contact the publisher.

For my family

INTRODUCTION

Money was no doubt a driving force for Madam C.J. Walker, the

Orphaned child and first free-born in her family. It gave her motivation to

Travel the country and sell her range of

Hair care products to black women who likely

Envied the attention and praise of long, straight hair. Her

Resilience made her rich beyond her dreams and able to help others. Her

Death left A'Lelia a glamorous but tragic heiress who became a patron of the

Arts and a *goddess* of the Harlem Renaissance. If you want to know more about it

U should read her great granddaughter's forthcoming book about her, the second

Generation of the Walker legacy, a legacy that came about despite racial

Hatred. Madam C.J. Walker and A'Lelia are a testament to the power of

Transcendence. Let their story serve as an

Education for us all, regardless of race or gender, so that there may be no

Regrets in our final days.

Sarah Breedlove/Madam C.J. Walker
Madam C.J. Walker Collection, Indian Historical Society

Lelia 'A'Lelia' Walker
Madam C.J. Walker Collection, Indian Historical Society

THE CHARACTERS

MADAM C.J. WALKER: Born Sarah Breedlove, the first free-born child to former Louisiana slaves in 1867, Madam C.J. Walker was orphaned at seven, married at 14, became a mother at 17, and was widowed at 20. After the death of her first husband, Moses McWilliams, Sarah moved to St. Louis with her daughter, Lelia, where she worked as a washerwoman for more than a decade, earning $1.50 a day. There she would meet and marry John Davis, an abusive alcoholic. The toll of stress during this time, plus long hours of backbreaking labor and a poor diet, caused her hair to fall out. She tried everything that was available, but without success. After working as a maid for a chemist, she invented a successful hair care formula and sold it across the country. Not only did she sell, she also recruited and trained legions of women as sales agents for a share of the profits. In the process she became America's first self-made female millionaire and she gave black women everywhere an opportunity for financial independence. On May 25, 1919, she died at her home in Irvington, NY of kidney failure. She was 51.

LELIA (A'LELIA) MCWILLIAMS WALKER:[1] Born in 1885, Sarah's only child would grow up to help run her mother's business. Relations between the two were complex and sometimes strained, compounded possibly by Lelia's speculated

---

[1] For most of the text I have used Lelia's given name, except where she refers to herself or in poems set after she changed her name to A'Lelia.

abuse at the hands of John Davis. Like her mother, the six-foot-tall Lelia married three times. An enthusiastic patron of the arts, she founded a culture salon that she called The Dark Tower. As its host she became a salonnière of the Harlem Renaissance as well as an intimate of its luminaries, whose opinions of her were not always rosy. Her close friend, photographer Carl Van Vechten, once wrote of Lelia that "she was too spoiled, too selfish, too used to having her own way to make any kind of compromise." Unable or unwilling to bear children, she adopted 13-year-old Fairy Mae Bryant, a local girl from Indianapolis who ran errands for Walker's sales agents.

FAIRY MAE BRYANT: Lelia noticed Mae during one of her visits to the Walker headquarters in Indianapolis. Mae had long thick hair and Lelia saw her as an excellent model for Walker products. They grew close, prompting Lelia to ask her mother, Etta Bryant, a poor widow with five children, if she could adopt Mae. Aware that Lelia could give Mae much more than she herself could, Etta consented. It is through the Bryant line that the Walker legacy is maintained to this day through Mae's granddaughter, journalist and author A'Lelia Bundles.

MOSES MCWILLIAMS: Sarah's first husband was a Mississippi labourer she met around the age of fourteen. Sarah married McWilliams to escape her cruel brother-in-law and "get a home of my own." McWilliams, like most blacks, took work where he could find it. When Lelia was two, he died in a mysterious accident.

JOHN DAVIS: Described by neighbors and acquaintances as 'fussy, mean, and dangerous', Sarah began a relationship with Davis after the death of one of her brothers and at one of the lowest periods in her life. They married when Lelia was nine years old. After they divorced, Sarah rarely spoke of Davis so very little is known about him besides allegations that he was a womanizing drunk who flaunted his lover in Sarah's face.

CHARLES JOSEPH WALKER: Sarah's third husband and business partner, Charles J. Walker was a reporter for one of St. Louis's three black newspapers. He was also a charmer and self-promoter who loved fine suits and well polished shoes. Sarah saw him as someone with whom she could build a future. But in the end, Charles couldn't handle a successful wife and when Sarah learned he was being unfaithful, she cut him loose.

ANNIE MALONE POPE-TURNBO: Or Madam Poro, as she was professionally known, was a manufacturer of hair care products and remedies, and someone for whom Sarah briefly worked. Poro claimed that it was her product that cured Sarah's stress-induced baldness, in contradiction to Sarah's story that it had come to her in a dream. Sarah would eventually eclipse Madam Poro after a brief but bitter rivalry.

PREFACE

Like any successful entrepreneur, Madam C.J. Walker was driven. How else as a black woman could she have become America's first self-made female millionaire during one of the most racially violent periods in American history? This fact leaves me chillingly inspired. As a mother, I've long been intrigued by highly successful working moms. Knowing that great achievement requires great sacrifice I wondered, what were Walker's sacrifices?

I started with this question, and it led to many more: What did money mean to Sarah? How did her daughter feel about their journey from rags to riches? What, if any, were the drawbacks of their wealth? Did Sarah's ambitions have an impact on Lelia's sense of self? Could the death of her own mother when she was a child have compromised Sarah's more nurturing instincts? And how did they really feel about their hair?

These are just some of the questions I explore in **Out of No Way** (which takes its title from an old saying in the African American community to 'make a way out of no way,' or to thrive against impossible odds), while also tracking the phenomenal rise of Sarah Breedlove into Madam C.J. Walker, of penniless orphan into the "wealthiest Negro woman in America."

I opted to tell her story through the lens of the mother-daughter relationship via different poetic forms, with each chapter addressing an issue relevant to their lives at that time. Written against the backdrop of Jim Crow, **Out of No Way** is ultimately an examination of what W.E.B. Du Bois called "conflicting identities." Sarah was a proud African American on the one hand and a woman seeking America's acceptance on the other. She was a pauper who achieved the American Dream while denied the rights and protections of the American Constitution. She was a wife, mother, and businesswoman who juggled the demands of family with the demands of work. And she was an orphan who had to transcend a painful childhood in order to be a good mother to her daughter. As Du Bois stated at the time, "One ever feels a two-ness. An American, A Negro… Two warring ideals in one dark body." Indeed Sarah Breedlove/Madam C.J. Walker was an American and a Negro, as was her daughter, A'Lelia, both of whom likely viewed herself through their own conflicting identities. What did they see?

R.A.

Sydney, Australia
27 December 2019

BOUKMAN

PRESS

CONTENTS

Money (Lyric)...2

Orphan (Narrative).............................16

Travel (Sonnets)...................................23

Hairku (Haikus)...................................36

Envy (Blackout)...................................45

Resilience (Speech)...............................86

Death (Elegy)..94

Art (Nursery Rhyme)..........................97

U... (Experiment)................................102

Generations (Couplets).......................104

Hate (Nursery Rhyme).......................109

Transcendence (Villanelle).................115

Education (Various Experiments).......117

Regrets (Various, Acrostic).................131

Afterword..136

Acknowledgements...............................143

About the Author.................................144

OUT OF NO WAY

ROJÉ AUGUSTIN

money

$0.70 — 1878
(Missus B— & Sarah)

Missus B—:

Seventy cents. Seventy cents will suffice. Mister B— will pay you seventy cents to clean the chamber pots and gather the body and bed linens. Do that first thing Saturday morning, mend any that need it, that includes the farmhand and his kin washing, too. On Sunday soak everything in warm water with soap. Oh that reminds me, you'll have to make more soap, enough to last the rest of the winter. Soak everything and add lye. Soak it all twice, see my fingers, two times. Come Monday morning get wood from the barn and rain water from the creek well, I suspect you'll need 20 or 30 gallons. Rain water is best because rain water is soft water, see? When you are set to washing put the clothing and the linens on the burlap, not directly on the ground, doesn't matter that they're already dirty, they're not ground dirty or dirty like you all, which reminds me, wear a clean linsey-woolsey, or an apron when you bring it all back. Make sure you employ, do you know what that means, girl, employ? Make sure you employ the four-stage method. When you turn the body linens inside out for the second wash, use fresh water for the second side, don't use the same water on the second side, understand? Boil the whites in soapy water, when they dry, three passes of ironing will suffice, you understand suffice? That means it will do, girl, three passes will do. Before all of that go to the general store near the Jessup farm and pick up a bag of sugar and some tea, tell the store boy to put it on Mr B'— account, he will know what. Now fetch those saddles up from the fence and bring them to the barn before you get the chamber pots. Bobby's going riding with… well, never you mind who just get them to the barn so Freddie can give them a polish. Tell him to get Little Skylark ready, too. My lord Sarah you are a strong one! How old are you, child? Ten? I have nev-

er seen a nigger girl shoulder three saddles at once! You will make a fine domestic, see? What? Don't you dare sass me. You should be thankful the good Lord has provided you with honest work to help your sister. My word. Do it like a good Christian and straighten your mouth before I make it bleed. Work, that's what a good nigger girl needs. Now go get the sugar and tea and bring them directly to Miss Lillie in the kitchen so she can check it's all there, understand? After that you can get on to the washing. When you have done all the chores as I have instructed, Mr B — will pay you your seventy cents, seventy cents will suffice...

$1.50 — 1898
(Missus F— & Sarah)

...it to say we need a new girl to cook the ladies luncheon tomorrow and Missus B — said you were reliable in the kitchen. We have nine coming so use the big pots down in the cellar, bottom shelf to the right. There is a crate of potatoes too if you could mash them up with some cream. Fish, I want, or fowl, vegetables from the garden, two sourdoughs; and think of something for dessert. When you're done with the cooking, polish all the silver to a high gloss, and I mean a high gloss. I need that done by twelve o'clock, service at one. I'll put the table linens in with the rest of the laundry after supper so wait til then, save you a trip. I have to say I am so relieved you were able to come so quick. Our other girl was...well I'm sure you heard...such a shame at her age too, only 13, and she claims it was a white man! Foolish child. Anyway, mind you wear a head wrap when you're in my kitchen. I'll pay you $1.50 for the supper and the usual $1.50 for the laundry. I have to say you are one of the best washer girls this side of the Missouri. I just wish...

...She would drop dead so that I can get on with my calculations, which If I have done correctly work out that my wages are up to $0.15 per hour, $1.50 per day. That's $9.00 per week, about $36.00 per month, $432.00 per annum. Lelia's schooling will need $7.85 for one month's boarding. At three months that's $23.55, plus $6 for her jacket and skirt, $1.75 for the shirtwaist, plus $0.20 per week for my night courses, five weeks, that's $1.00. Night courses Lord yes, thanks to that new class of St. Louis Negro I am meetin' at church. Men with professions. Elegant women wearing fine hats and frocks. I do as they say, take me some night courses to better my lot. Lord knows I am fed up with the $1.50 a day I get for washing the soiled laundry of white families whose women are so weak they can hardly take the linens off my hands! And I know that if...

.. there were more like you. My mother-in-law took one look at my linens and asked me straight away who my washer girl was and I told her Sarah Davis! The best washer girl in St. Louis!...Pray you don't get ravaged like that other girl. I am just too tired to look for anymore help. Anyway, never you mind that. As long as...

...John is messing around with that Suzie girl and giving her his wages, I am on my own. Come home from work, tired and hungry, and he has the nerve to soil my table with whiskey bottles and cigarettes. It's thanks to his drinking that he contributes nothing except heartache, and vexes me something fierce when I count the few pennies we have left at the end of each month. I grabbed those bottles, I grabbed them off the table and threw every last one to the floor! Felt good. But I have to keep John for now because there is never enough; have to get what I can from him in the most unChristian way when I quietly step up to wherever he has thrown his trousers and run my hands through the pockets. It's often that I find nothing cept a crumpled cloth but sometimes there are coins thank Jesus, or one or two notes and I always only take half — that's the Christian in me. Lord his fists rained down on me like a storm when he saw all that broken glass. But I stood firm. I said, "John, I know you are giving money to that harlot! Shame on you when you have a wife and a child, and an empty cupboard. Nothing but dirty work that you need to beg and borrow for, not to mention the constant threat of being out on the streets!" The worst thing about that night was my Lelia. How she trembled so. Clinging to me, tears in her eyes. How she buried her face in my neck and sobbed while that brute cornered us with his rage. But I held firm, for my baby. Poor child can't understand why we are forced into a prison of poverty for no reason other than the color of our skin. But good Lord…

…you behave like a good Christian, and keep your legs closed, you'll be fine. Now be sure to give my washing the four stage method. Some of the Irish girls say they do but I can tell they're lying! I tell them, you have to do it like the coloureds do. Turn the body inside out for a proper scrub, use fresh water on the second side then boil it. And always three passes of ironing…

…the blood stains…the blood stains in Mister F—'s shirt-waist…how they haunt me. And the mountain of laundry I have before me now…so much I can't help but weep and wonder what will become of me when I grow old? What am I going to do when my back gets stiff? What am I going to do to better my condition…?

Walnut Street — 1899
(Lelia)

...of where we live. When I came home from delivering Mrs M —'s linens on Thursday I found a white lady waiting at my doorstep with questions about my school attendance. Where is your mother she wanted to know? I told her at work, not home, and could she come back tomorrow after school. She said she could but then followed me upstairs anyway and that's when I stopped breathing. If you're wondering why it's because she would see how we live — the too many people in a two-room house, with three on the floor and two in the bed: my uncle, his wife, mother, me... and *John*. Not my father. Laundry too, hanging in every corner. And socks on the floor. Shoes by the door... If she really wants to know about my absences, I'll tell her look around and see for yourself how it is when my mother has so much work and how I try my best to help her keep up. I do some washing. I mend the holes. I tidy the room. I cook when she can't. I even help her with her hair. On the rare occasions that I find myself unnoticed — and this is sometimes a luxury don't get me wrong — I sit and look out the window where all I see is hard working women everywhere, doing their best to cope and it makes me weep. Because hatred is our prison. Because the whites fill me with rage. But then John stumbles in stinking of whiskey. The lust in his eyes so hot and vile I have to leave the room. If the W.C. isn't free, which is often, I go down to Frankie's because both her neighbors were shot down in Chestnut Valley. Frankie's a few years older than me and treats me like I'm grown. She has a fella named Al who is eighteen but acts like a tyrant and won't let her be. She asked me once what I would do if I had money like white folks and I told her I would get us away from John, that's the first thing! Then I'd buy us a house with plenty of privacy in it, and I'd hire a girl to wait on my mother so she wouldn't have to work all the time.   And I would buy us a shoppe's worth of frocks, one for each day, that someone else could wash and mend. And a cook too, who would plate us our meals six days a week. Some new boots would be nice, the kind that buckle straight up to the knees. I'd have lots of big parties and I would wear a turban, yes a turban! Made of velvet and gold lace, with moonstones on the front, and a Peacock's feather! There are girls at my school from the 20th Century Girls' Club whose fathers are barbers or newspaper men and whose mothers organize and speak at church. Those are the girls I would invite to my parties. Lord knows that would feel mighty good...

$275,937.88 — 1919
(Sarah)

...of you to wrap up this perfume, while I try on this hat and that brown suit in the window on the left-hand side, also those pumps over there, and whatever else you think I may need. Oh, and if you find one in my size, three camisoles in silk please, but not in white, and did we pass umbrellas on the right? One of those as well. Add a few towels, the thirstiest you've got. And the linens won't be too much, unless of course I buy the lot, good Lord excuse me, this cough is really sticking to me, but to answer your question one thing I did not expect were the begging letters, so many, every single day, asking for money in every single way. I do my best to help where I can but there are just so many. Yes, I'll take that too, wrap it all up please I'm tired and I would like to go home and rest, which reminds me, my dream of dreams is finally complete! My new house! You must pay us a visit. It has a pool and a garden and 34 rooms. There's also a Chickering that is perfectly tuned, and the Estey, my organ, piped all through the house, and Aubussons, Battenburgs, and fine Haviland china. The most stunning things, not to mention my books, all housed on four and half acres of what Tandy calls "verdant green nooks." I wanted plenty of room in which to entertain my friends, oh dear excuse me, this cough is really sticking to me. What's that, the Spanish flu? It's bad, I know, but we will get through. For now I think I should like to rest for a while. Yes do come for dinner when you can. Enrico Caruso came for a visit and said that I ought to give my house a name.   "Madam," he said, "call it Lewaro, Lewaro, Villa Lewaro." I looked at him and then he explained — it was my baby. My darling baby, Lelia Walker Robinson.

Le. Wa. Ro. See? So when you stand outside and take it all in, you will know what a monument it is to colored girls every- where, a monument…

Le. Wa. Ro. — 1919
(Lelia)

12

...is what mother calls it, but it is the *things inside* that thrill me, the *things* that throw their light across my shadows. The few dozen things of monogrammed silver that beam so bright, the Tiffany things that glow like gemstones in the night, the jewel things with their brilliant hue things and the cars, big sexy things that do their gleam thing, my dream of dream things! But yet, I regret that no one warned me how quickly these dream things would fade into no-thing, how the thrill of *things* would blur into a strange boredom. I became beautiful but bored, and now I find that my things do nothing to my shadows, they are merely sharpened and darkened and cast in high relief...

Debt — 1930
(Lelia)

...is nowhere to be found. In the garden, although they say the garden will be lost, despair has begun its march into night and into the huge standing open spaces off the kitchen, where the dinner things have been sold, with the shadows on the platters and the dull uncovered teapot, the water boiling and the curtains being drawn across the windows where the buyers in their suits and frocks and pearls are turning the tags to see the cost of the platter and the teapot and the boiling water and... my Lord this headache is blinding... but the garden, the garden will sleep tonight, turning off all its private moons, and they say it will be lost and that we can no longer walk through it. Still we mustn't end shedding light on this nightmare by the pool and the gazebo and the lounges, the lifting and dropping of the windows in the kitchen and your face never to be at those windows again, waiting silently for me and the opening and closing of your mouth that will never utter another word. It is Thanksgiving, they said Thanksgiving. It is Thanksgiving and the buyers don't want to know that they were bested so I remain hidden, just looking around at the unending dread of so great a loss as this...

...There is nothing but poverty ahead, this headache is blinding me, they said Thanksgiving was best because people are more generous at Thanksgiving so we auctioned everything off and now there is nothing but your ghost inside the house, making the empty rooms echo more loudly in my ears, and the loss of your tender spectre across the floor makes the dark fill up the cracks in hard sharp spasms of loneliness, turning my joy into dust before my very breath. But if my own shadow isn't dust already or in a slow rage then it may never be, God this headache is blinding! If I remain still, the floor will turn into your lifeless face, mother, cracked, crumbling and ancient. Forget everything they say, this headache is *blinding*, could you have left this place and abandoned me? Where will you be tomorrow?

Madam C.J. Walker's Villa Lewaro in Irvington-on-Hudson, NY
Madam C.J. Walker Collection, Indian Historical Society

orphan

Graves & Thrones[2]

Act One

We are at Battle Creek Sanitarium, 27 November 1917. Evening.
The crackle and pop of a fire is heard. It is warm and imploring and
telling of words like 'listen' and 'care.'
The curtain rises. Before us is a suite that comprises
A grave-like bed and a throne-like chair.

Lelia, my precious child, I understand your thoughts run wild.
But now that we are both reconciled, consult my tale to not bemoan.
Finer in life, you are, you see, unlike so many born unfree.
Do not lament "could mother be?" — "could mother be?" is not known
Give thanks for what you are not — a motherless child without a home,
Nameless grave, nor empty throne.

When my parents died so vainly, there was forged a space so plainly,
Of undying incompleteness, for which my soul could scarcely atone.
I was but seven years old, remember, when faced with true terror
At the sight of the Grand View bearers, now orphaned and alone.
Standing on that deathly field, I now recall what it made known:
Scores of graves, and ghostly thrones.

Wracked was I with grief, and robbed, and mourning of the loss, I sobbed
A long brutal year's worth of tears for both to rebound as flesh and bone.
Rarely a moment came my way of love or warmth that urged me stay.
Despite my dreams of whiter days, family round hearth, this well known,

---

[2]The structure and meter of Graves & Thrones is modelled after Edgar Allan
Poe's *The Raven*

Sealed was my fate to be a penniless waif without a home,
Born of graves, and buried thrones.

There I sank into a well so miserable — vulnerable!
Wholly unutterable! — scraped and soiled like a neglected moonstone.
Made to feel an unperson, and seeing that my lot did worsen,
I found my heart had coarsened, my lucent girlhood notions thrown
By merciless night shadows delivering the serpent's own
Wicked grave and shameful throne.

All that was left was to self-destruct, then begin to reconstruct
An unyielding self that was stronger, yet sombre, and rapidly grown.
Uncertainty became my friend, and fear a devil to transcend.
Become *someone!* — a Godsend! Whom no one ever dare disown!
A Lady, a *Madam*, with all the treasures my dreams had shown,
Neither grave, nor buried throne!

For what is damnation but to seek from others validation?
Inward was my diligence thrown, orphan to die and Madam to hone.
With hard work, both day & night, I repaired my wounds and made things right.
For us, I harnessed the sheer might of forebears whose wings had flown.
And when I glimpsed within — a vision of gold that brightly shone
August grave, and stately throne.

Thus my path became one of resilience, fierce independence.
Borne upon the blackened ashes of grief and loss and a strong backbone.
I resolved to be a problem-solver, for I had you, my daughter.
A child to safeguard from squalor, polish to a *rich* Moonstone.
And for me, an orphan's deep ambition to build my own home,
My own grave, and my own throne.

If I am cold, t'is self-protection, take this not as rejection.
Take it all with much self-reflection, and see me as your stepping stone.

Left with a sister and four brothers, but how to be a mother?
Forgive me this, my lips now utter, "mother" remained unknown.
For my travels on the road, for which I left you much alone,
Dig *that* grave, bury *that* throne.

Lelia, my only child, I understand your thoughts run wild.
But now that we are both reconciled, consult my tale to not bemoan.
Finer in life you are, you see, unlike so many born unfree.
Do not lament "could mother be?" — "could mother be?" is not known.
Remember who you are — a blessed child with glorious homes,
Honoured graves, and noble thrones.

Act Two

We are still at Battle Creek Sanitarium, 27 November 1917.
Evening. The maelstrom and rush of water is heard. It is cold and
confronting and telling of words like 'temper' and 'dread.'
The curtain rises. Before us is a suite that comprises
A throne-like chair and a grave-like bed.

Sarah, my earnest mother, who well provided like no other,
For now that we are both reconciled, I heed your tale to not bemoan.
Right you are that I not complain, nor point to you with any blame.
Gratitude I give for the many gains your dreams have thus shown.
But utter I must "could mother be?" — *Mother* went long unknown.
Distant grave and solemn throne.

When my father died so suddenly, I was left so utterly
Terrified — that I would, by the cruelties of life, be soon disowned.
I was but a young girl, full of fright, when my young mind did ignite
With such an innocent light, that ours was now "fatherless" home.
And with you in grief, the attention I sought was little shown.
Father's grave and vacant throne.

There followed many difficult years, many nights of secret tears,
Uprooting and moving and moving so often like leaves lost and blown.
T'is true we did not quarrel much, t'was often we would sit not touch,
As if there was no attachment as such, like a missed milestone.
An important foundational seed never properly sown
As clod to grave, gem to throne.

My gravest was John Davis, from whom the Lord in time did save us.
He spooked me with his rough cruel hands, shifty eyes, & drunkard's baritone.
Was then I hated life the most, wanted only to be a ghost.

He would see just my ghost, not my mouth, my legs, nor private zone.
But instead might treat me as my father had—a rare moonstone,
Born of earth and fixed in throne.

During this time I felt great shame, and felt as well so much inflamed.
As though I was not sufficient enough, nor favoured to be well grown.
No place to rest my feelings, t'was all consumed by your own healing.
Your song to *be someone!* pealing, drowning out my undertone
Of pressures, perfections, and great expectations all my own
Shallow grave and shameful throne.

Yet still I learned to overcome, as not to be a girl undone,
To follow your ambitious road of darkly glittering precious stones.
Yet one problem you could not foresee: thorns of guilt inside of me.
For many recoiled who thought me spoiled, your *rich* moonstone.
I was born and ensconced in a world between orphan and throne.
Mournful grave, and stately home.

You talk of being orphaned like only death can make an orphan,
But what of your "not now, I'm working"? My being sent away from home?
I understand more than you think, for from this well I also drink
A bitter brew of hoodwink, and living in motherless homes.
You who were hardly there even while you were must now atone
For jilted graves, vacant thrones.

Orphaned mother, lonesome child, the reason for my thoughts so wild?
As I could have none of my own, Mae I adopted so we would be known
For more than the wealth that left me torn, one side rose, one side thorn.
Forgiveness, from which I am shorn, shows me now that *heart* is home.
Not Sarah Breedlove's grave, nor Madam CJ Walker's throne.
Heart is the seat of my throne.

My dear earnest mother, who well provided like no other,
Yes now that we are both reconciled, I heed your tale to not bemoan.
Right you are that I not complain, nor point to you with any blame.
Gratitude I give for the many gains your dreams have thus shown.
But whisper I must "could mother be?" *Mother* remained unknown.
Shadow grave and lonely throne.

Travel

The Lost Letters, 1905 - 1908

July 1905
My darling baby,

I am Westward to Denver, in search of opportunities
Aboard a steam train I shall call Reinvention.
It whistles the promise of new communities
And dreams of my ascension.

You will know I hear the engines roar
And breathe the fire of Jim Crow steam.
But in that fire my heart does soar
Knowing what to our race it means.

My bag is filled with Turnbo tins!
My mind with lush anticipation!
I feel that West is where ambitious winds
Will greet me at the station.

Oh Lelia, travel bestows such adventure,
There isn't a place I would not venture!

Your devoted Mother

July 1905
Dearest Mother,

Are you leaving me for Denver?
For those treasures to unearth?
To best Jim Crow and the scorn it renders?
To remake yourself and reclaim your worth?

I know well what it is you leave behind,
A brutal life of meagre wages.
I hope and pray that the dreams you find
Shed light upon our darkest rages.

Safe journey, mother, and ready your tins!
Remember I am thinking of you back home,
As you set sail on those ambitious winds
Armed no doubt with your brush and comb.

Your strength will carry you with zeal and pluck,
I wish the very best for you, good luck!

Love, Lelia

May 1906

Oh Lee, a year's work I've been doing now
And I have done so for my teacher.
But the pupil in me now must bow
As that pupil becomes the teacher.

I spend two days per week on washing,
And five days doing Poro hair.
But my dreams gave visions of root dressings
That far effectively grows hair.

My own has grown to splendid length,
Proof to each new customer.
Their endorsement gives me further strength,
They can see I am no hustler.

Should I part ways with Annie?
Do please answer me quickly.

Hugs and kisses,
Mother

May 1906
Mother,

Is this not the reason you left home?
To follow your heart's ambition?
You are wise to venture on your own,
Have no guilt or doubt in this decision.

The more you sacrifice our time
The more I shall expect in return.
I'm not talking about a nickel and dime,
I'm talking about money that burns.

Can you earn paper like the white man?
Can you change our lives for something better?
Are you sure it will all go to plan?
Can you promise all of this, mother?

Forgive me if I sound hopeless.
It's just so lonely in St. Louis.

Miss you, Lelia

June 1906
My darling baby,

I think often of our unstable years,
How you had the grace to endure without complaint.
But I may yet calm your present fears
With this grand picture you will help me paint.

I have found that I am a gifted talker,
And already enjoy some fame.
And now that I am Mrs C.J. Walker,
My products will bear this name.

You must come before Christmas.
I will need your capable hands.
I can put you in charge of the office
While Charlie and I crisscross the land.

Come as soon as you can to Denver.
Can you arrive before September?

                    Hugs and kisses and kisses, Mother

July 1906
Dearest mother,

I will arrive on the 23rd of August!
I hope that my hands will do you proud.
I have studied the hair course as promised.
And will do all I can to build your crowd.

I am so very excited now!
I can see your picture in greater detail.
To you, my new teacher, I will certainly bow.
The moment I alight the Missouri Rail!

You are right, travel bestows much adventure,
Adventure for which I would gladly die.
True, there is not a place we shouldn't venture,
Nor one we shouldn't also bid goodbye.

Three weeks wait will be very tough,
August cannot get here soon enough!

With love, Lelia

January 1907
Dearest Lelia,

Are you happy, are you well installed?
Are you managing the parlour?
Your earnings leave me quite enthralled,
I am convinced we can grow larger.

There are more Alabama girls to train,
A lot more money to be making.
I have nothing but dollars and hair on the brain!
A feeling that all is ours for the taking!

I know you will continue to have great success
While you run the parlour on your own,
It does certainly put you to the test,
But I am confident you will build your throne.

So as not to leave my knowledge short
Be sure to send a full report.

Much love and kisses, Mother

April 1907
Dearest Mother,

There is a hornet's nest of lies about.
Poro agents are claiming that we are thieves!
And now Annie has her claws drawn out
At our business to slash and cleave.

What do you propose we do,
To stop this turning into scandal?
Would you like me to push on through,
Or close up shop and take a gamble?

I can't bear being here to deal alone.
Won't you please hurry back to Denver?
I need the support of your strong backbone
To put this feud to bed forever.

I am worried about her accusations.
They could cause us complications.

Yours, Lelia

May 1907

Lelia, make a brief announcement
That our parlour will close and move elsewhere.
Let us counter Annie's denouncement
By doing what is just and fair.

Besides, Colorado's black population is quite small,
There is limited potential for financial growth.
I have felt, in fact, that we would hit a wall,
So now we must find new markets for us both.

To do this I must travel more
Through the growing cities South and North.
My sales have already begun to soar
From canvassing both back and forth.

Don't worry, you can sleep well tonight.
Everything will be alright!

Love,
Mother

June 1907
Dearest Mother,

Now that the Denver shop is closed
When shall we meet again?
I agree with the plan you have proposed;
Where next should we go and when?

I can meet you in the North.
Up there seems especially ripe.
Then return back East by Feb the fourth
So we can do as you described.

I agree, Pittsburgh is best for our headquarters,
The train lines spread like branches.
From there we can manage all the mail orders
And increase our national expansions.

Let me know your rail line,
I will arrange to meet you there on time.

Travel safe, Lelia

July 1908
Oh Lelia,

I saw bodies hanging in a tree today,
I saw the anguish of those who grieved.
I saw the guilt of whites held not at bay,
I saw the cold wilderness of thieves.

I saw a grin that caved my heart.
I saw bitter tears through burning breath.
Why Lelia, do they rip our lives apart,
And throw upon us wanton death?

I saw spilled the blood of innocence.
I saw torn the flesh again and again.
I saw them kill God's citizens.
I saw the hate of evil men.

The whites must hate themselves so savagely
To act with such barbarity.

With a broken heart, Mother

The lynching of Virgil Jones, Robert Jones, Thomas Jones, and
Joseph Riley. Gelatine silver print. July 31, 1908, Russellville, Logan
County, Kentucky. Photographer Unknown

hairku

Sarah's Hair

My hair was young, free.
Mamma's fingers danced through curls,
Tat braids with ribbons.

Sunday she was gone.
No longer here to plait hair
By the morning light.

Caught shadows of me.
My hair is *not* unruly,
Just thinks for itself.

Mister on his horse.
Head wraps dot like strange cotton
In the August heat.

Soft hairs are like flames
Lit only by Gibson's Girl.
My envy burns there.

Long work at the tubs.
No point to check a mirror
For negro women.

St Louis mirror.
My panicked heart goes racing!
Hair fall and bald patch!

ROJÉ AUGUSTIN

Searching everywhere
For a cure to grow it back,
I try *everything*.

Then comes a woman
With a business of her own
Growing negro hair.

She is Miss Annie.
I learn everything I can
To be just like her.

"Part the hair in fours,
Mix the ingredients well.
Massage into scalp."

Repeat.

Repeat some more.

Using Poro cream,
I quickly see a new scheme.
There begins my dream.

Work bore little fruit
Until I woke from dreaming
Of African roots.

Filled my room with fumes;
Packets of strange and dark herbs.
Grew my own hair back.

Natural hair growth

Gives the promise of freedom
Ever in my name.

Lifting as I climb
With the only thing I can,
My God-given hair.

Lelia's Hair

Ma unwraps my scarf,
Parts my hair into sections,
Drags her comb through, ouch!

Through the torn curtain
Combing knots sends my curls down
On the kitchen floor.

Hot comb on the stove.
Crackle of heat through my frizz.
She won't let me be.

Ma at the mirror,
Fretting with her reflection.
Hair becomes her life.

Stink of sulphur fumes
And cayenne pepper powder
Bought from root pedlars.

Women cloaked in white.
Swish and gloop of mixing creams
Every Saturday.

Soft little edge swirls,
"You've got good hair, Fairy Mae,"
I envy you that.

"Try our new shampoo.

(Your money back guaranteed)
Will cure your tetter."

Or:

"Try our new glossine.
(Your money back guaranteed)
Will make your hair shine"

Or:

"Vegetable shampoo.
(Your money back guaranteed)
Natural hair pap."

Suitcase by the door,
Ready with preparations.
Barely says goodbye.

Grand Harlem salon.
Women wait and sip French tea.
The wealth that hair built.

ROJÉ AUGUSTIN

Why Our Hair is not Straight

Our hair is not straight
Because we are not straight, no
We curl with laughter.

Our hair is not straight
Because we are not straight, no
We twist into song.

Our hair is not straight
Because we are not straight, no
We bend in prayer.

Our hair is not straight
Because we are not straight, no
We wave and frizz on.

Our hair is not straight
Because we are not straight, no
We curve while dancing.

Our hair is not straight
Because we are not straight, no
We swirl with high hopes.

Our hair is not straight
Because we are not straight, no
We circle like crowns.

Our hair is not straight

Because we are not straight, no
We braid and we cope.

Our hair is not straight
Because we are not straight, no
Ask God up above.

She will tell you:

"Their hair is not straight
Because they are not straight, no
They coil in my love."

James VanDerZee, Tea Time at Madame C.J. Walker's Beauty Salon.
Gelatine silver print, 1929. Copyright © Donna Mussenden VanDerZee

envy

The Voice in Her Head

Envy the girl with irresistible beauty, whose skin is flawless
and velvety, whose hair has a beautiful silky sheen, the girl
who receives glances of undoubted admiration.
Envy her
beauty...
Envy her lovely hair
and her charming complexion.
Remember the
Appearance of the hair?
Irksome now. Today there are
Thousands of them, everywhere,
The length, thickness, texture
Recognized the best.
Astonishing
Hair...
Long, luxuriant tresses.
They
Have held high rank
A real wish to become her.
Learn how.
Glorify the womanhood of our Race
Daily stimulating the
Growth, increasing the length, softening and thickening
short, stubborn, unsightly hair;
If for no other reason,
Know the merits of
Loud praise. Learn how.
Enhance your beauty, make you admired by men and the
envy of

Women. Today, now. Hope.
Have long, luxurious
Hair and a beauty-kissed complexion.
One's skin is a bar to employment
Opportunity
…for colored people
The peculiar texture of Race hair and skin.
Our entire race
Do you want a good job?
Have you short, thin
Unsightly hair?
You owe it to yourself to
Prepare for any
Emergency in life.
Become a beauty.
Earn your own money.
Be independent.
Is your skin
Ugly?
Nothing counts
Against one so much
As
Skin.
You want Beauty of
Complexion and loveliness of
Hair
Countless thousands of women throughout America have
Priceless beauty and
Incomparable chic and charm
To their hair and skin. These women
Succeed almost everywhere.
These women.

Are these beauties more wise than you? Then do as they do, go,
Look for the sign.
Throughout the world, superior
Women,
Indescribable beauty of hair.
You won't forget.
Velvety smoothness, admirably attractive.
Positively nothing like them that provoke unending com-
pliments.
—Leaders in society tell us,
There is a difference.
Do as these women do, get the habit.
Look for the sign.
The key to happiness and success is a GOOD APPEAR-
ANCE
You are often judged by how you look.
As you walk down the street—when you go to church or to
entertainments—notice the people
about you. Unconsciously you pick out those who are more
pleasing and attractive.
Half the battle of achieving success is to look successful. The
other half depends upon your
Determination, your ability. Remember that and go!
Personal cleanliness, neatness, whitened teeth, luxurious
hair, clear complexion, nice
Hands—these are important points
To
Great work.
In fact, it
Invigorates, stimulates new
preparations
with Mme C.J. Walker's

inventions
As the
Mme. C.J. Walker system.
There is nothing imaginary about Mme. C.J. Walker's
Preparations. Genuine.
A great deal of expense to put these preparations up
With the Walker trade-mark. Genuine
Mme. C.J. Walker Preparations.
There is an old saying that woman's crowning glory is her
hair, and
I have
To say
Women everywhere are
Wonderful.
A million eyes turned daily
everywhere.
Supreme in reputation.
Wonderful hair
Everywhere in U.S.A.

Sculptures of Envy

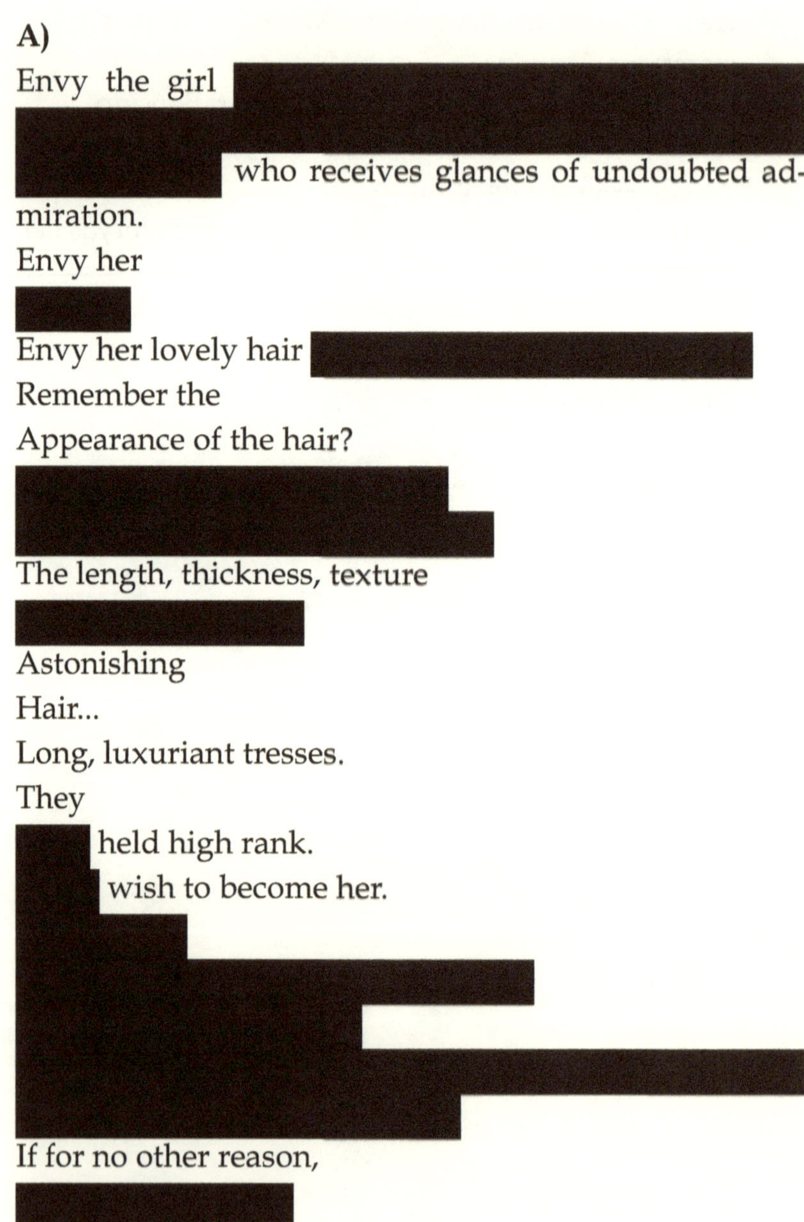

make you admired by men and
the envy of
Women. Today, now.
Have long, luxurious
Hair and   beauty

Do you want a good job?

in life.

Is your skin
Ugly?
Nothing counts
Against one so much
As
Skin.

These women
Succeed almost everywhere.
These women.
Are these beauties more wise than you? doubt it.
do as they do,
Look for the sign.

You won't forget.

provoke unending
compliments.

Do as these women do, get the habit.
Look for the sign.

GOOD AP-
PEARANCE

As you walk down the street—when you go to church
or to entertainments—notice the people
about you.

Remember that and go!

Everywhere in U.S.A.

B)

Envy the girl
Who receives glances of undoubted admiration.
Envy her

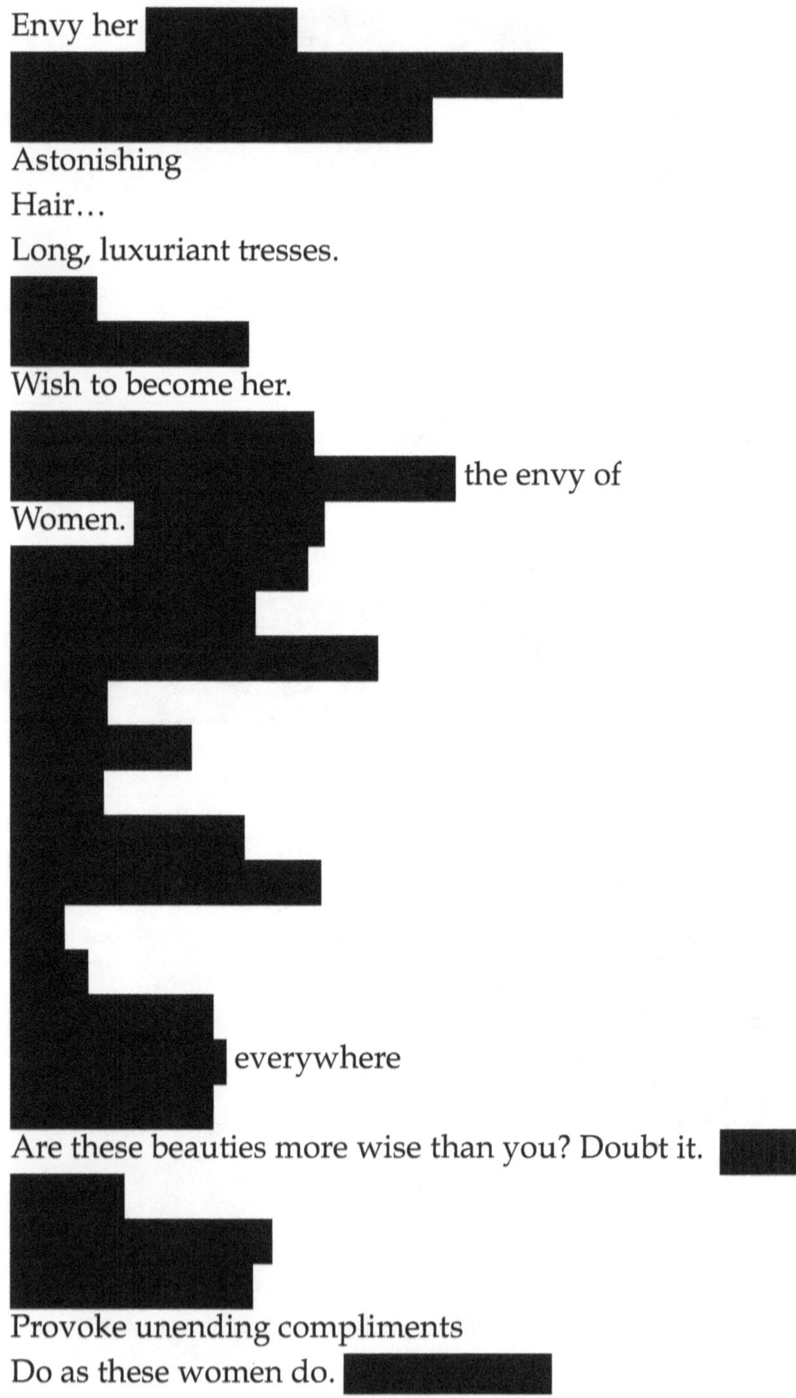
Envy her

Astonishing
Hair…
Long, luxuriant tresses.

Wish to become her.

the envy of

Women.

everywhere

Are these beauties more wise than you? Doubt it.

Provoke unending compliments
Do as these women do.

Look for the sign.
GOOD APPEARANCE
███████████████████████████
███████████ —notice the people
About you.
███████████
Everywhere in U.S.A.

C)
Envy the girl
Who receives glances of ███████ admiration.
Envy her.
Envy her.
Astonishing
Hair…
Long, luxuriant tresses.
Wish to become ███
The envy of
Women
Everywhere.
███████████████████████████
███████████████
███████████
Look for the sign.
GOOD APPEARANCE
███████████
Everywhere in U.S.A.

D)

Envy the girl

Envy her.
Envy her.

Wish to become
The envy of
Women
Everywhere.

Everywhere in U.S.A.

E)

Envy
Envy her.
Envy her.
Wish to become
The envy of
Women

Everywhere in U.S.A.

F)

Envy.
Envy her.
Envy her.

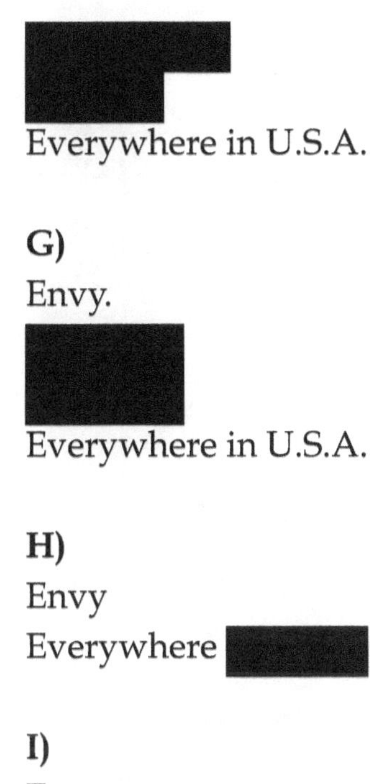

Everywhere in U.S.A.

G)
Envy.

Everywhere in U.S.A.

H)
Envy
Everywhere

I)
Envy.

Ad No. 2—3 Columns x 150 Lines=450 Lines

Madam C.J. Walker Collection
Indiana Historical Society

1) "You too may be a fascinating beauty"

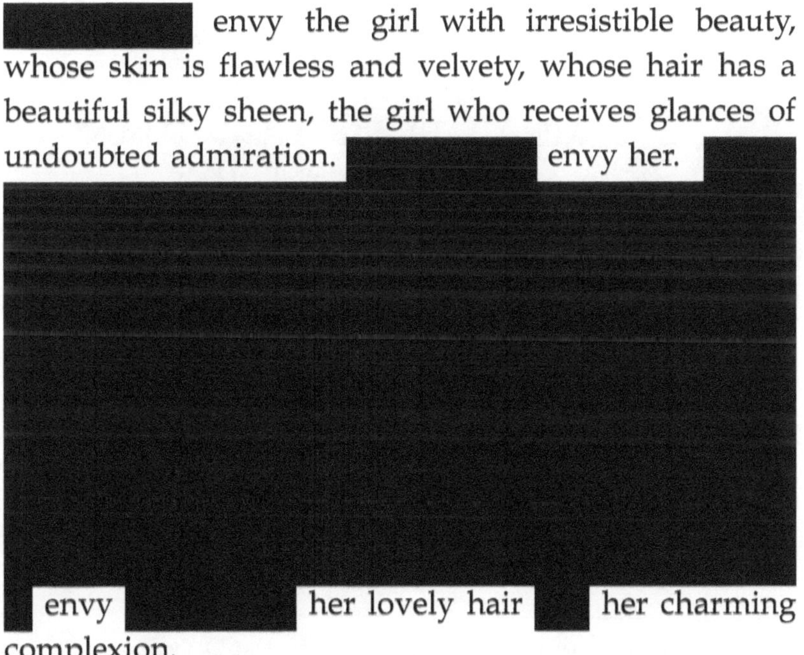

██████████ envy the girl with irresistible beauty, whose skin is flawless and velvety, whose hair has a beautiful silky sheen, the girl who receives glances of undoubted admiration. ██████████ envy her. █████

████ envy ██████████ her lovely hair ███ her charming complexion.

Madam C.J. Walker advertisement, 1923. Chicago Defender.
"What a Change a Few Years Make."

2) "What a Change a Few Years Make"

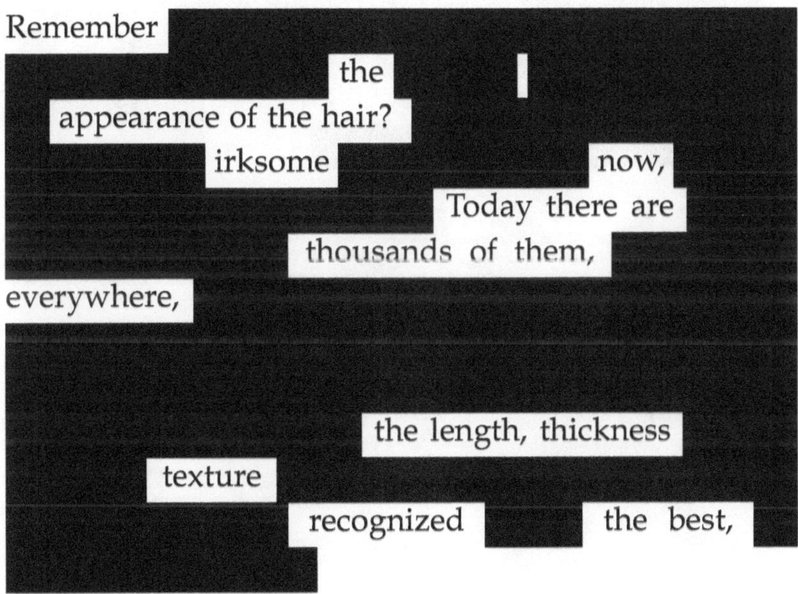

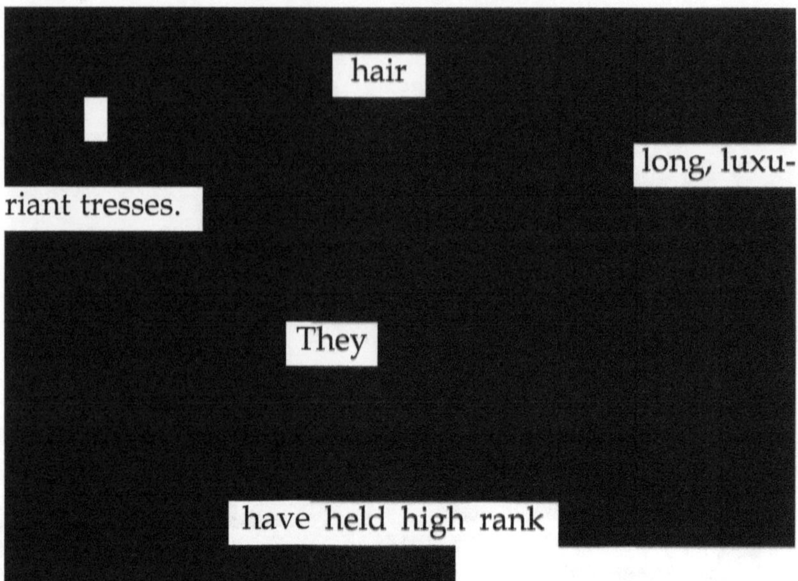
hair
long, luxu-
riant tresses.
They
have held high rank

Madam C.J. Walker Collection
Indiana Historical Society

3) A Real Opportunity for Women

Madam C.J. Walker Collection
Indiana Historical Society

4) "Glorifying Our Womanhood"

glorify the womanhood

of our Race

by

daily

stimulating the growth, increasing the length, softening and thickening short, stubborn, unsightly hair; clearing complexions, smoothing, softening and preserving skin.

if for no other reason,

know the merits of

loud

praise

learn how

enhance your beauty, make you admired by men and the envy of women.

today, now.

have long, luxurious hair

and a beauty-kissed complexion.

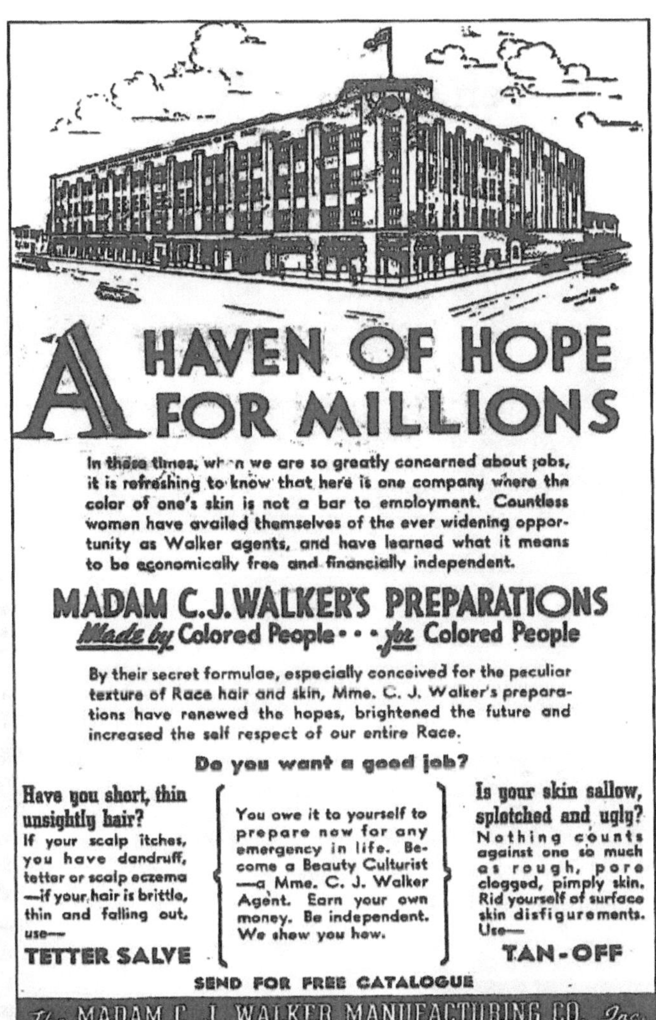

Madam C. J. Walker advertisement, 1920s: "A Haven of Hope for Millions" (Madam C. J. Walker Collection, Indiana Historical Society)

Madam C.J. Walker Collection
Indiana Historical Society

5) "A Haven of Hope for Millions"

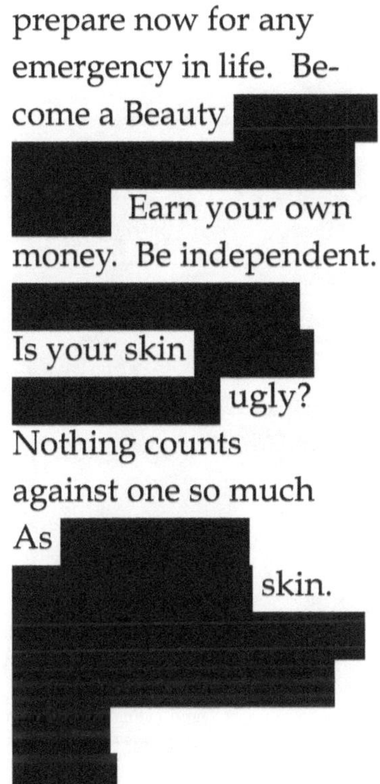

prepare now for any
emergency in life. Be-
come a Beauty

Earn your own
money. Be independent.

Is your skin

ugly?
Nothing counts
against one so much
As

skin.

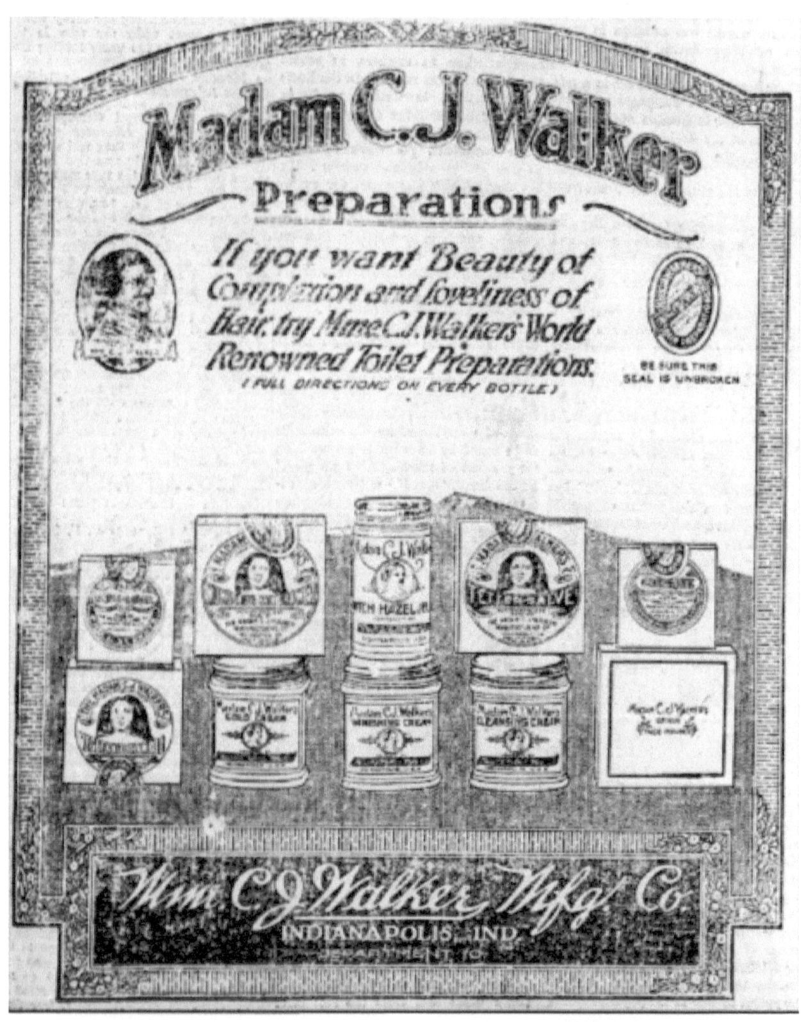

Madam C.J. Walker Collection
Indiana Historical Society

6) Madam C.J. Walker Preparations

you want Beauty of
Complexion and loveliness of
Hair,

Madam C.J. Walker Collection
Indiana Historical Society

7) "A Wise Choice"

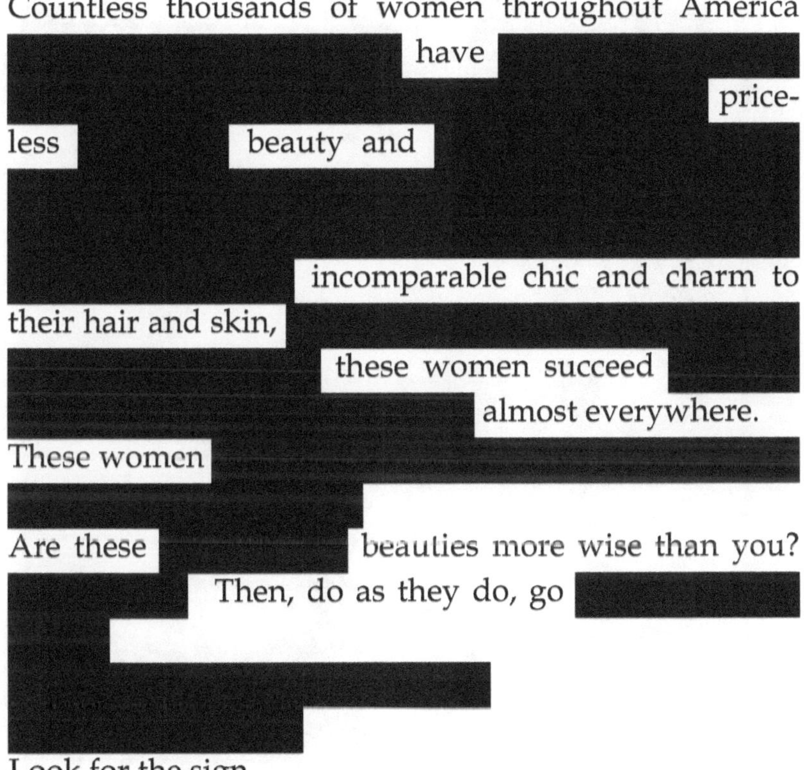

Madam C.J. Walker Collection
Indiana Historical Society

8) "Their's is the Magic Touch"

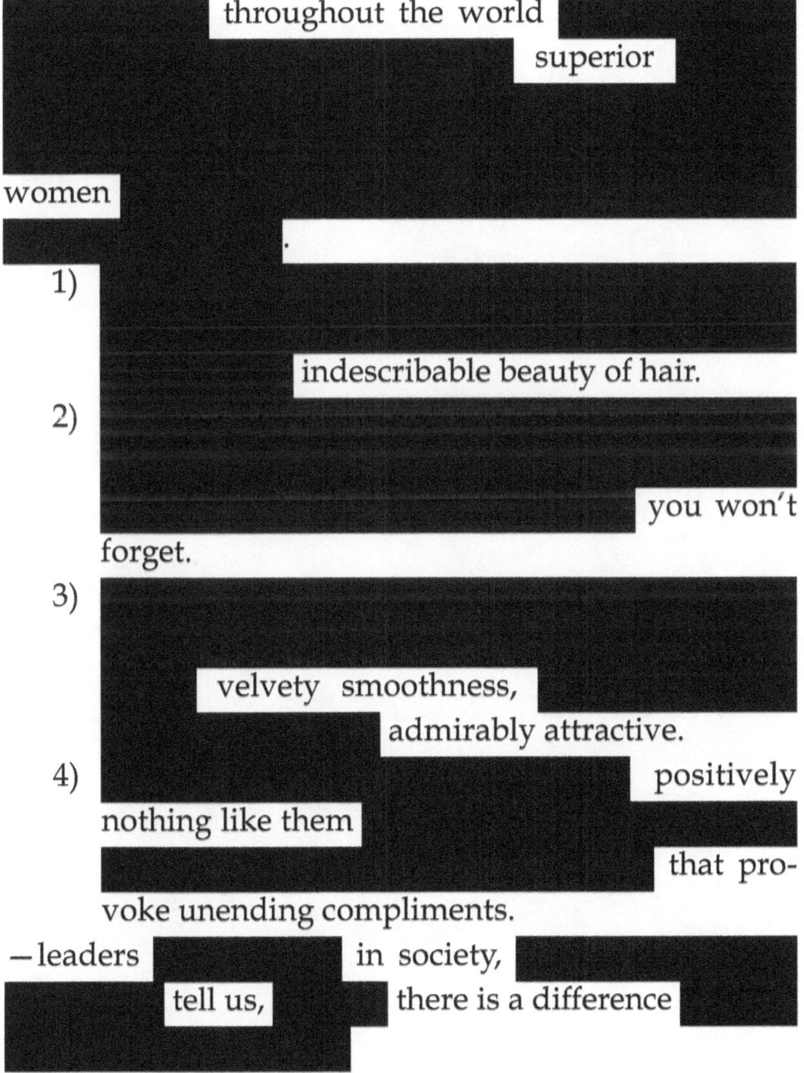

Do as these women do, get the habit

Look for the sign.

Madam C.J. Walker Collection
Indiana Historical Society

9) "Madam Walker Often Said"

"The key to happiness and success is a GOOD AP-
PEARANCE
You are often judged by how you look"

As you walk down the street—when you go to church
or to entertainments—notice the people about you.
Unconsciously you pick out those who are more pleasing and attractive. █████████████████████████
████████████████████████

Half the battle of achieving success is to look successful.
The other half depends upon your ████████ determination, your ability.   Remember that ████ and
████ go ████████████ Personal cleanliness, neatness,
whitened teeth, luxurious hair, clear complexion, nice
hands—these are important points.

███████████████████████████████████ to
██
██
██
██
███████████ great work. ████████████████████
██

Madam C.J. Walker Collection
Indiana Historical Society

10) "Madam C.J Walker's Preparations for the Hair"

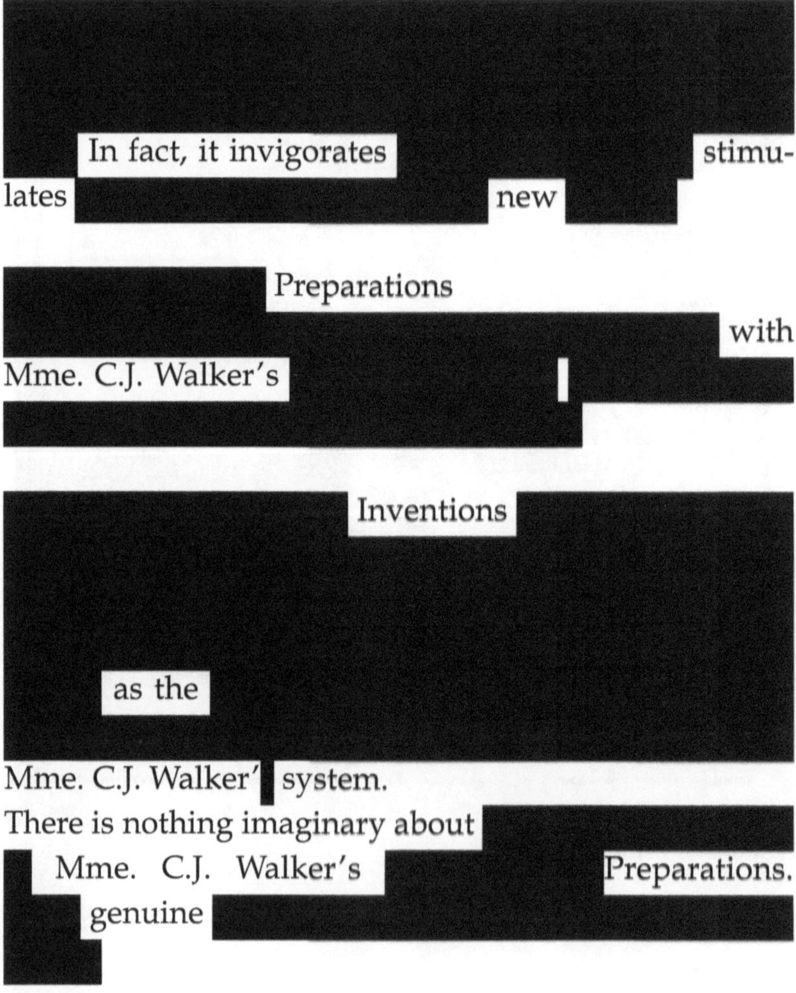

a great deal of expense to put these
preparations up
with the Walker trade-mark
genuine Mme. C.J. Walker Preparations

Madam C.J. Walker Collection
Indiana Historical Society

11) Beautiful Hair "Women's Crowning Glory"

There is an old saying that woman's crowning glory is her hair, and I have to say

Women everywhere are

Wonderful

84

Madam C.J. Walker Collection
Indiana Historical Society

12) "A Million Eyes Turned Upon it Daily"

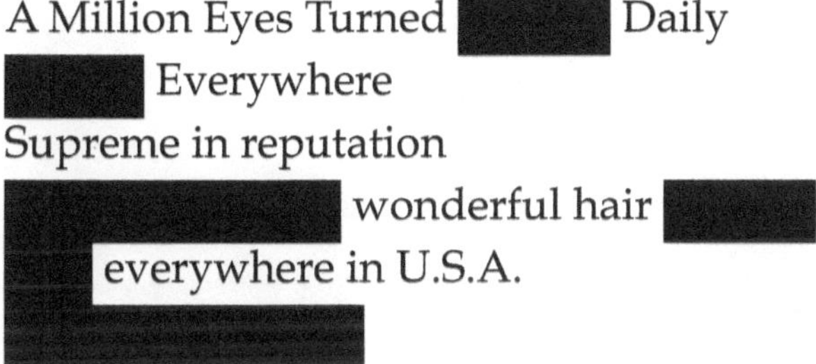

resilience

"Resilience: Making a Way Out of No Way"
Speech by Madam C.J. Walker
Given at the Anti-Lynching Conference of June 1918[3]

Ladies and gentlemen, thank you, thank you for joining me here today. I am here to speak out against the horrors of lynching, which continue to take place across this nation, and how we may continue to stand firm against such horrors. I want first to start by telling you of an incident that took place in Brooks County, Georgia.

It begins with Hampton Smith, a 31-year-old white plantation owner who was well known for abusing and beating his workers. His reputation as a violent boss was so widespread that it became increasingly difficult for Smith to find workers. To solve this problem, Smith turned to debt servitude, the practice of leasing convicts by paying their bail in exchange for their labour. It was in this way that a young man by the name of Sidney Johnson — who had been arrested and fined $30 for rolling dice — came to be working on Smith's farm. After only a few days in the fields, Smith beat Johnson and withheld his pay for not working on a day that Johnson was sick.

Fed up with the abuse — and no doubt with a system that had brutalized him since childhood — Sidney Johnson shot and

---

[3]This speech is a work of fiction by the author. However, the stories of Sidney Johnson and Hazel and Mary Turner are true.

killed Hampton Smith out of desperate rage. He then fled. A lynch mob quickly formed to hunt down Johnson and any others who crossed the mob's path. The manhunt lasted more than a week, during which time at least a dozen innocent negroes were rounded up and killed.

One of those innocent victims was Hazel Turner, a married father of two who had previously worked on Smith's plantation. He and Smith had had an altercation earlier in the year, after Smith beat Turner's wife, Mary. Turner was arrested and sentenced to several months on a chain gang for daring to defend and protect his wife. When the manhunt for Sidney Johnson set off, Hazel Turner's previous conflict with Smith made him an all too easy target, and so he was summarily apprehended and lynched.

Distraught by the murder of her husband, Mary Turner publicly and courageously denounced the killing, maintaining Hazel's innocence. She declared that she would get the names of those responsible and bring them to justice. Outraged that a negro woman would have the audacity to challenge white authority, the mob decided that Mary needed to be "taught a lesson" for her "unwise remarks," as the local newspapers described it.

And so, on Sunday, May 19, the day after her husband's murder, Mary Turner, mother of two young children and eight months pregnant with her third, was captured and taken to Folsom's Bridge on the Brooks and Lowndes County border. NAACP investigator Walter F. White described what followed. Mrs Turner was tied and hung upside down by her ankles. Her clothes were then soaked with gasoline and burned from her body. Her belly was slit open with a knife like those used for splitting hogs, exposing her unborn child. The infant fell to the ground and gave out two feeble cries before a member of the mob viciously stomped it to death with the heel of his boot. The mob then riddled Mary's body with gunfire. She and her baby were buried just ten feet from the site of their horrific murder. A whiskey bottle with a cigar stuffed in its neck was used to mark the makeshift grave. Despite a full report being given to Georgia governor Hugh Dorsey, which included the names of the instigators and more than ten other participants, not a single person was brought to justice.

So, I am here today on behalf of Mary Turner, whose murder is but one in the long, dark history of brutality against the American negro. Her lynching serves as a stark reminder that our bodies have become a scapegoat for white guilt.

Before emancipation, the negro in America was seen as a docile, childish creature content with service to his master. After the proclamation, when the negro was finally declared free, he quickly became a "monster" in the eyes of white America. Words like "criminal," "savage," "indolent," and "ignorant," are often used to describe us. But I ask you here and now, who is the true "monster" in Mary and Hazel Turner's nightmare? Or in Sidney Johnson's? Or in any of the countless victims of lynch mobs? In a sense, you could say that when whites talk about the American negro in such vile terms, they are really talking of themselves.

Consider that the purchasing of human flesh and the cramming of that flesh onto a fleet of slave ships only to land them on the shores of a hostile foreign world to be enslaved, impoverished, dehumanized, robbed, beaten, raped, and killed for the purposes of commerce, control, and entertainment is monstrous in the extreme. Consider that the refusal to uphold the values of morality, kindness, and respect for all of God's creatures is utter savagery. Consider that forcing others to tend your homes, cook your meals, wash your laundry, and raise your children without adequate compensation is a mark of gross indolence. And finally, consider that the systematic and widespread abuse of political, economic, and judicial power to strip the American negro of his freedom and humanity is not only a criminal act but also an ignorant one, for it causes as much damage to the oppressor as it does to the oppressed, only in different forms. For the oppressed, the damage is self-evident. For the oppressor, it gives rise to a violent and divided society where the unbridled pressures of injustice rise to a level of self-destruction. White supremacy is the moral ignorance that will destroy America if left unchecked.

Knowing full well the dire consequences of "stepping out of line," I don't know a single negro who would knowingly, willingly, break the law, or cross a white man, woman, or child if given the choice. I don't know a single one who would risk the ensuing rampage for anything short of survival. Therefore, the persistent claim that the American negro is thusly a threat is a lie.

When the civil war ended, negroes had a beacon light of hope in the reconstruction of the South. But that hope proved to be short lived as the fear, guilt, and resentment of southern whites took hold. Klan terrorism aborted justice and begat Jim Crow, a new mask for the same grotesque face of racism.

Until white Americans admit that their wealth and privilege are due not to genetic superiority or divine favoritism, but entirely to the violent exploitation of the American negro, there will be no peace, for as far as I can tell white privilege is the most pernicious force America — indeed the world — has ever known, and racism its most pernicious stain.

But we must not despair. We must make a way out of no way. And we do this with resilience, because the American negro is nothing if not resilient. It is in our blood. If we are to overcome the maladies of this nation — the lynchings, the cross burnings, the shootings, the intimidation, the disenfranchisement, and the exploitation — much resilience will be needed. And what exactly is resilience you may ask.

It is the strength of character that allows us to rebound from trauma. It is facing life's most difficult challenges with the courage and the wisdom of a disciplined warrior. It is having a clear sense of justice, and the vision for a better tomorrow. It is community and relationships, to which we give and turn for support. It is a determination to enjoy the self-evident truths of our great declaration of independence — that we are *ALL* created equal, that we are endowed by our Creator with certain unalienable rights, among these are life, liberty, and the pursuit of happiness. We can not allow these times of deep division and hate to dishonor the tremendous wisdom of that declaration.

I was orphaned at a young age not just by the death of my parents but, like all negroes in America, by the estrangement from my heritage. Yes, I suffered abuse. I was married young, and had a child at seventeen. I became a widow at twenty. There followed many back-breaking and lonely years of washtubs and meagre wages. Of uncertainty and fear. But despite all of this, despite Jim Crow, despite not having the right to vote, despite the daily campaign of terror against my people, I promoted myself from an orphaned child to a businesswoman, from a slave cabin to a thirty-four-room mansion, from utter destitution to bountiful luxury. And I did this by the grace of resilience.

So, I am here today to say that if your hearts ache from the atrocities taking place out in the counties of America, if the cruelties of life overwhelm your faith, then say aloud and say it proud: We are nothing if not resilient! We can make a way out of no way! Let us all take action and do what we need to do henceforth. Let us give ourselves the respect and dignity we deserve. And let us never turn away from our hardships but face them squarely, like disciplined warriors.

I offer these words today as a requiem for Mary Turner and her child, for Hazel Turner and Sidney Johnson, for the returning black servicemen who fought valiantly for this country only to be killed on home soil for daring to wear their uniforms in public, indeed for all those whose lives were destroyed by acts of fear, guilt, and greed. With our resilience we honor your death.

And finally to those whose deeds perpetuate injustice, whose hearts are filled with hatred, and whose hands strike out in violence, I ask only this: Of what are you so afraid?

Death

Elegy for My Mother — 24 May 1919[4]

Mother…
From the ship, I dream of you mid-ocean.
You appear in the bosom of spring.
The buds around you are warm,
The land awakens from winter's sleep.
Your ghost springs forth just like this:
Bare hands, bare feet,
Eternal life that is light and warm forever.

Near to your heart,
A phoenix soars across the blue skies.
A journey beckons like a beguiling snake.
You worship its fruit.
The life of a seller is given to her buyer
At love's expense.

For you it will be the first night unlike yourself,
A night of reapers and truth.
The hidden parts of your soul give in,
The scope of your heart is full,
Laughter surrenders in you,
The stillness of your thoughts succeeds,
And you stay your enemies.

Tomorrow you will walk through the garden.
You will be poised under a familiar coldness,

---

[4] A'Lelia Walker was traveling at sea when she received news that her mother
was dying. Though she tried with everything at her disposal, she was unable
to make it back home in time to say goodbye. She was reportedly devastated.

OUT OF NO WAY

To lose your grief out in the cities,
And be praised over and over again.
The shadows of your grieving heart
Are drawn from the blood of your veins.

In the small silences of today,
Where the mourners weep,
Angels in the temple of heaven know
That I, who have been left behind,
Carry the mighty weight of repentance
Above all.

Water, give up your tortured waif!
Madam C. J. Walker has died!
While I on this vessel cry,
Taking refuge in the cradle of her legacy.

The dream of light,
The angels of heaven,
The eternal seas,
All revealed in love.

Tomorrow we will walk through the garden.
We will be poised under a familiar coldness,
To lose our grief out in the cities,
And be praised over and over again.
The life of a brave woman
is rooted in the soil of her death.

Art

The Salon that Art Built — 1927

This is the salon
  that art built.

This is the patron, A'Lelia Walker,
Who hosts the salon
 that art built.

This is the poet Countee Cullen,
Who charmed A'Lelia
Who hosts the salon
 that art built.

This is the playwright, Langston Hughes,
Who smoked with Countee
Who charmed A'Lelia
Who hosts the salon
 that art built.

This is the writer, Zora Neale Hurston,
Who danced with Langston
Who smoked with Countee
Who charmed A'Lelia
Who hosts the salon
 that art built.

This is the singer, Alberta Hunter,
Who sang for Zora
Who danced with Langston

Who smoked with Countee
Who charmed A'Lelia
Who hosts the salon
    that art built.

This is the activist, W.E.B. Du Bois,
Who laughed with Alberta
Who sang for Zora
Who danced with Langston
Who smoked with Countee
Who charmed A'Lelia
Who hosts the salon
    that art built.

This is the composer, Nora Holt,
Who clapped with Du Bois
Who laughed with Alberta
Who sang for Zora
Who danced with Langston
Who smoked with Countee
Who charmed A'Lelia
Who hosts the salon
    that art built.

This is the novelist, Jean Toomer,
Who spilled Nora's drink
Who clapped with Du Bois
Who laughed with Alberta
Who sang for Zora
Who danced with Langston
Who smoked with Countee
Who charmed A'Lelia
Who hosts the salon

that art built.

This is the photographer, Carl Van Vechten,
Who snapped Jean's portrait
Who spilled Nora's drink
Who clapped with Du Bois
Who laughed with Alberta
Who sang for Zora
Who danced with Langston
Who smoked with Countee
Who charmed A'Lelia,
Who hosts the salon
    that art built.

This is the designer, Paul T. Frankl,
Who toasted with Carl
Who snapped Jean's portrait
Who spilled Nora's drink
Who clapped with Du Bois
Who laughed with Alberta
Who sang for Zora
Who danced with Langston
Who smoked with Countee
Who charmed A'Lelia,
Who hosts the salon
    that art built.

This is the painter, Aaron Douglas,
Who argued with Paul
Who toasted with Carl
Who snapped Jean's portrait
Who spilled Nora's drink
Who clapped with Du Bois

Who laughed with Alberta
Who sang for Zora
Who danced with Langston
Who smoked with Countee
Who charmed A'Lelia,
Who hosts the salon
     that art built.

A hundred more guests, the darlings of
Harlem!
Were regaled all night!
And mingled with Aaron
Who argued with Paul
Who toasted with Carl
Who snapped Jean's portrait
Who spilled Nora's drink
Who clapped with Du Bois
Who laughed with Alberta
Who sang for Zora
Who danced with Langston
Who smoked with Countee
Who charmed A'Lelia
Who hosts the salon
     that art built!

U...

Is This U?

Unloved
Unarmed
Unbroken
Uncertain
Uncomfortable
Unconquerable
Unconscious
Unconventional
Undaunted
Undermined
Underpaid
Underprivileged
Unbreakable
Undervalued
Unforgettable
Unhappy
Unhealthy
Unheard
Unpredictable
Unrelenting
Unselfish
Unshakable
Unsung
Unwanted
Upbeat
Upset
Upstanding

Is this U?

Generations

Conversation in Couplets

Madam C.J. Walker: Daughter, did I on you too often self-project?

Lelia Walker: Little Mae, barren I must be, so you must pass on our legacy.

Fairy Mae: Mama, will you with Miss Lelia and Madam let me go?

Madam C.J. Walker: Many beautiful things, how does it feel to now have all of this?

Fairy Mae: Why, Lelia, did you change your given name?

Lelia Walker: At times you did but it earned me great respect.

Fairy Mae: I will Miss Lelia, of course. I will do it for posterity.

Etta Bryant: I will my child, with an ache that only a mother can know.

Fairy Mae: Oh Madam, where once I had needs, now I have bliss!

Lelia Walker: I wanted here, as in Paris, to be known by a grand name.

Lelia Walker: Great granddaughter, what would you say to me in this moment?

Madam C.J. Walker: Ah yes, gratitude! Let me give thanks to you, daughter, for your love and support.

Lelia Walker: Mae, as it is the reason we met, I give thanks for your beautiful hair.

Madam C.J. Walker: Little Mae, I give thanks for the honor of being your grandmother.

Fairy Mae: A'Lelia Bundles, although we never met, I give thanks for your birth.

A'Lelia Bundles: Thank you, Grandmother, I am told you were salt of the earth.

A'Lelia Bundles: I would say, great grandmother, that I am so grateful for your bestowments.

Lelia Walker: And let me give thanks to you, mother, for a throne at your court.

Fairy Mae: Miss Lelia, I give thanks to you for adopting me and making me your heir.

Fairy Mae: My dear Madam, I give thanks for the honor of being your granddaughter.

Madam C.J. Walker: Great great granddaughter, I give thanks to you, keeper of my flame.

A'Lelia Bundles: And I give thanks to all of you supreme women for dignifying our name.

Hate

"Great men cultivate love and only little men cherish a spirit of hatred; assistance given to the weak makes the one who gives it strong; oppression of the unfortunate makes one weak."

— *Booker T. Washington*

Birth place of Sarah Breedlove/Madam C.J. Walker
Photographer unknown

The Prison of Racism that Hate Built

There is a prison of racism
that hate built.

There are people
Lynched in the prison of racism
that hate built.

There was a woman
Who helped the people
Lynched in the prison of racism
that hate built.

There was Jim Crow,
Which angered the woman
Who helped the people
Lynched in the prison of racism
that hate built.

There were white men
Who created Jim Crow,
Which angered the woman
Who helped the people
Lynched in the prison of racism
that hate built.

There was a system
That rewarded the white men
Who created Jim Crow,
Which angered the woman

Who helped the people
Lynched in the prison of racism
that hate built.

There is a government,
That built the system
That rewarded the white men
Who created Jim Crow,
Which angered the woman
Who helped the people
Lynched in the prison of racism
that hate built.

There was a president,
Who headed the government
That built a system
That rewarded the white men
Who created Jim Crow,
Which angered the woman
Who helped the people
Lynched in the prison of racism
that hate built.

Here is America,
That elected the president
Who headed the government
That built a system
That rewarded the white men
Who created Jim Crow,
Which angered the woman
Who helped the people
Lynched in the prison of racism
that hate built.

There is the NAACP,
Who challenged America
That elected the president
Who headed the government
That built a system
That rewarded the white men
Who created Jim Crow,
That angered the woman
Who helped the people
Lynched in the prison of racism
that hate built.

There was the money
For the NAACP
To challenge America
That elected the president
Who headed the government
That built a system
That rewarded the white men
Who created Jim Crow,
That angered the woman
Who helped the people
Lynched in the prison of racism
that hate built.

Here is the woman,
Madam C.J. Walker,
Who was born in America
And defied the odds
To make the money
That gave her the wealth

To live and help
Free the people
Lynched in the prison of racism
    that hate built!
    Amen, sister!

transcendence

Fear is the Devil We Must Transcend

Fear is the devil we must transcend.
Transcend is what Madam Walker taught.
May our deeds point bravely to that end.

Those ravaged by fear can not ascend.
The heights of self that can't be bought.
Fear is the devil we must transcend.

To not transcend is the truth to bend.
Transcend by truth is what she taught.
May our deeds point bravely to that end.

And what is truth but a selfless friend?
A selfless friend that is never fraught.
Fear is the devil we must transcend.

The noble thing is to transcend.
What fearful ones so cruelly raught.
May our deeds point bravely to that end.

Be brave, said Madam, and thus transcend!
Let all our demons come to naught.
Fear is the devil we must transcend.
May all our deeds point to that end!

115

Education

"We went every day about nine o'clock, with our books wrapped in paper to prevent the police or white persons from seeing them... After school we left the same way we entered, one by one, when we would go to the square about a block from school, and wait for each other."

— *Susie King Taylor, who attended a secret school in Savannah Georgia circa 1850s.*

Lelia, Knoxville College 1902 - 1904

Reading

I remember as a child how mother knew
That reading could spring our lives anew.
Her soul grew yearning for those things
That we were told only fit for kings.
Yet books revealed within a glimmer,
A heavenly light of freedom shimmered.
For freedom's way, she learned to read
What law forbade compelled by greed.
The words she read by night alone,
The books she purchased on her own,
Those lessons gave her life more meaning,
What helped her soul indeed was reading.
From Douglass, Du Bois, and Booker T,
All gifts of wisdom they came to be.
Like a vessel that carried her across the shore
Where bells of freedom rang once more.
She held the books she read so dear,
The knowledge contained within so clear.
It was as if her mind was bathed in light,
For the pages she read ensured her flight.
It was learning to read that dissolved the lie,
Un-clipped her wings and bade her fly.

Question: What is truer than truth?
Answer: A Story.

— Ancient Proverb

Writing

Notes on writing:
Take notes
To write is to write is to write again...
If you wish to sharpen the mind
Write/revise while ???? your pen/again??
??...kind / find...
If you wish to perfect/project?? your mind??
What is writing?
Vocabulary
Grammar
Structure
Prose
Poetry
Story
Language
Words
Saying something
                    To write...

DRAFT ONE

To write is to write is to write again
Taking care to revise again and again
Work out the idea, give/develop?? a structure/a picture??
Whether poetry or prose, must have a structure
Go through the grammar, as if with a hammer
Claw out the words that don't matter
Nail down the punctuation nail down the conjugation
Improve/increase?? your vocabulary
Command the language learn lots of words
Then enjoy the glory
Of having written a story
Like a lump/body?? of clay
You cut and mould and tease out all day
You mould and you tease out what you want/need?? to
say
Like a lump of clay
Tease out what you want to say
Like a body of clay
Tease out what you need to say
Layers of work done a day at a time...

DRAFT TWO

To write is to write is to write again
Taking care to revise again and again
Work out the idea and give it a structure
Sentence upon sentence, build up a picture
Like a sculptor at play with a body of clay
Mould and tease out what you need to say
Layers of work done one day at a time
Cutting out words or finding a rhyme
Nailing down the grammar
As if with a hammer
Checking your conjugation
Checking your punctuation
Increase your vocabulary
Avoid sounding ordinary
Whether poetry or prose
Treat your words like a rose
Then you can enjoy the glory
Of having written a story

DRAFT THREE

To write is to write is to write again
Work out your idea and give it a structure
Take care to revise again and again
Word after word, as you flesh out your picture

Like a sculptor at play with a body of clay
Layers of work done one day at a time
Mould and tease out what you need to say
By cutting out words or finding a rhyme

Nail down the punctuation
Nail down the grammar
Nail down the conjugation
Be brutal with your hammer

Daily Increase your vocabulary
Whether it be for poetry or prose
To avoid sounding ordinary
Treat your words like a rose

It is then that you will know the glory
Of having written a story

DRAFT FOUR

To write is to write is to write again.
Taking care to revise again and again.
Work out your idea and give it a structure,
Word upon word, you build up your picture.
Like a sculptor at play with a body of clay,
Mould and tease out what you need to say.
Layers of work done a day at a time,
Cutting out words or finding a rhyme.
With a syntactic hammer
You nail down the grammar;
You check the punctuation,
And you check the conjugation.
You improve your vocabulary
And you make it extraordinary.
Whether for poetry or prose,
Select your words as you would a rose.
It is then that you enjoy the glory
Of having written your story.
To write is to write is to write again,
Taking care to revise again and again...

"Knowledge makes a man unfit to be a slave."

— *Frederick Douglass*

Arithmetic

1) *Minerva picked six acres of cotton in one day. At this rate, how long will it take her to pick twenty-one acres of cotton?*
- Three days
- Four days
- Three and half days
- Four-and three-quarter days

2) *Owen, a negro slave who is one score and ten years, costs $360. As time goes on and Owen ages, his value depreciates by $45 per year. What is the value of Owen after nine years?*
- Four hundred and five dollars
- Forty-five dollars
- Minus forty-five dollars
- Four dollars and five cents

3) *After whipping Sarah, an overseer tells her to return to her work washing the laundry. He warns her that if she does not finish by sundown, he will whip her for five minutes each day for the first week and increase that time by one minute per day each week thereafter. How many weeks will it take to reach a twenty-minute whipping?*
- Three
- One

- Twenty
- Two

4) *Robert Burney sold two female slaves for every five male slaves he sold. If he sold ten female slaves, how many male slaves did he sell?*
- Forty-five
- Twenty
- Twenty-five
- Ten

5) *Over the course of one week, a lynch mob hangs twelve negroes on the first day, shoots ten negroes on the second day, and burns eight negroes on the third day, and so on in the arithmetic sequence. How many negroes does the lynch mob kill in a week?*
- Forty
- Forty-three
- Thirty
- Twenty-two

"The older I grow, the more I am convinced that there is no education which one can get from books and costly apparatus that is equal to that which can be gotten from contact with great men and women."

— *Booker T. Washington*

Notes on Black Power, ca. 1902 - 1903

-Pursue equality:
>(Declaration of Independence)

-Whites know that without education the American negro would cease to exist beyond the realm of white supremacy:
>(ex: burned schools, lynched teachers, jailed students...)

-Maintain quest for education. Stay educated:
>(A tradition of educational self-help in the negro community)

-Self-help/Self Improvement:
>(Cultivate self-awareness, knowledge of self)
>(First education is self-awareness)
>(Be self-aware, be educated)

-Give back:
>(Serve others)

-Cultivate a community:
>(Give and get support)

-Surround oneself with great people:
>(Best education)

-Never stop learning. Ever.

regrets

Poems of Regret

Read by A'Lelia Walker at The Dark Tower Poetry Evening
9 November 1927[5]

Poem One

The Dreamer's Wake

> Remember…
> Regretful themes
> Lie in between
> The gain and loss
> Of fabled dreams,
> > For
> The choices we make
> my never seem
> At first to be
> The dreamer's wake.

---

[5] This is a work of poetic fiction by the author.

Poem Two

To My Three Ex-Husbands

John, Wiley, James...
I regret I could not make it last,
The union we had, which came to pass;
I mourn the heights we both once flew,
A height that we so briefly knew.
My ways were selfish I suppose,
Like thorns that grew to protect a rose.
Yet now that you are all truly gone,
Regret creeps in each morning's dawn.
Am I cursed forever to never find
A lover's grace or peace of mind?
I mourn our union, which came to pass,
I regret I could not make one last.

Poem Three

Mother & Daughter

Money was indeed a driving force for my mother Sarah Breedlove, the

Orphaned child and first free-born in her family. It gave her motivation to

Travel the country and sell her range of

Hair care products to black women who likely

Envied the attention and praise of long, straight hair. Her

Resilience made her rich beyond her dreams and able to help others. Her

Death left moi, A'Lelia, a glamorous but tragic heiress who became a patron of the

Arts and a *goddess* of the Harlem Renaissance. If you want to know more about it

U should read my great granddaughter's forthcoming book about me, the second

Generation of the Walker legacy, a legacy that came about despite racial

Hatred. Mother and I are a testament to the power of

Transcendence. Let our story serve as an

Education for all, regardless of race or gender, so that there may be no

Regrets in our final days.

OUT OF NO WAY

Afterword

Want to make God laugh? Tell her your plans! This is one of my favourite quotes, and yes, I modified it. I include it here because this strange little poetry book was born out of shattered plans, or as I like to think of it, out of no way. I had never planned to write a poetry book. If anything, it planned itself.

I started writing this collection in the spring of 2018, after one of the most tumultuous periods of my personal and professional life. When I think back on it now, the tumult had been twelve years in the making, starting in 2006 when my husband and I migrated from my native New York to London, with our two-year-old daughter in tow.

There I became a 'stay-at-home mom,' a role I wanted. I always knew I would have children and I vowed that when I did — and if I could — I would cut back on work to raise them. Thanks to my husband's unwavering support, I was able to do exactly that. I spent most of those years in London indulging in the realities of motherhood, a gift I am grateful for. In 2008 we were blessed with a second bub and I was again lucky enough to do the same with her, this time in my husband's native Sydney.

I'd said goodbye to my life in the northern hemisphere, to my family and friends, and to a budding career as a writer and television producer. My plan at this point was to break into scripted television (a long held passion of mine), with the help of Aussie friends and acquaintances in the industry.

Australia would become the place where my daughters would lay down their roots, where my husband would settle into the role of provider, and where I would unwittingly begin a 10-year ramble as a "stay-at-home-mom-who-was-also-working-on-a-creative-project-with-the-hope-of-reviving-her-career-when-the-kids-were-old-enough." Needless to say, this is also where the tumult would begin.

What I didn't know when we moved to Sydney was that compared to America the size, diversity, and financial resources of Australia's television industry is tiny, which made it extremely difficult to break into, especially as a foreigner. I tried all sorts of ways to get my foreign foot in the door. I published a book, for starters. I joined the guild, I took refresher courses, I attended networking events, I entered script competitions, I signed up for mentoring programs, and I sought tons of advice from those aforementioned friends and acquaintances in the industry, many of whom did their best to help.

But in the end, I would spend the better part of ten years working independently, sometimes collaboratively, but always unpaid, on self-generated projects that I hoped would resuscitate my withering career. By the summer of 2017 the reality set in that no matter what I did, the economics of scripted television were stacked against me. I was an interloper in a very small pond, treading water with a glut of native swimmers. I would have to ditch my precious plan and set out in search of a raft.

In June 2017, I took a job as a producer on a panel show. Its audience wasn't huge, but it was a well-known and well-respected program. My first full-time salaried role in nearly thirteen years. I was terrified but also extremely grateful to get it. The job itself was enjoyable and stimulating. Largely self-directed, plenty of research, lots of interviews, lots of pitch and script writing, and the occasional field shoot. It suited me perfectly.

But as can often be the case in working life, the culture did not. It was rather like wearing a beautiful pair of shoes that killed your feet. I had a shared desk in the newsroom. It was very loud, and we were all packed in like sardines. Between myself and my nearest colleagues was a mere two and a half feet, on all four sides. As one of perhaps three brown faces in the newsroom, I was also very lonely, and at least ten years older than most of my colleagues, nearly all of them young, blond women. After ten anxious months I quit, my confidence and self-esteem in shreds.

June 2018, the winter of my discontent. By now I had fully awakened from the dream of "stay-at-home-mom-who-was-also-working-on-a-creative-project-with-the-hope-of-reviving-her-career-when-the-kids-were-old-enough" to the nightmare of being unemployed and pushing fifty. I had none of my New York peeps to turn to, I had none of my old friends and colleagues to ask for help, nothing of my culture to take refuge in, and no solid professional network to speak of. Despite an Ivy League degree, I felt completely dependent on my husband. I desperately looked for more options but found there were very few left. *How* had it come to *this*? When I had a plan. How had I become such a *failure*? These words, and worse still, dominated my thoughts for months, dragging me headlong into my sunken place. It was dark down there. I hit the bottom hard. And my poor husband, bless his heart, bore much of the impact with me. I was now back to square one.

As I mentioned earlier, I had for years been working independently on creative projects. One of those projects was about Madam C.J. Walker. I hadn't learned about Walker until I was in my 20s, and when I did my jaw literally dropped. Why hadn't her story been told in schools, I wondered. I became passionate about Walker, terribly in awe of her legacy. In many ways, I needed her. As a young girl, it would have helped me tremendously to know that a woman like Walker existed.

I'd researched her life for some time and had early stages of a spec treatment and pilot script when a friend called one day to tell me that a U.S. production company was in pre-production on a limited series about Walker for Netflix. I was both gutted and thrilled by the news, a strange brew. Gutted that I wasn't going to be a part of bringing her story to the screen as I'd hoped to do, but thrilled that it would finally get the recognition it deserved. When it came down to it, I didn't really care who was spreading her gospel, so long as it was being spread. But I had all this research that I'd devoured, and several drafts of a treatment and script that I'd worked on for months, plus hours and hours of my imagination devoted to her.

My friend suggested that I repurpose all of that work into a poetry book. My first thought was, *'why on earth would I do that?'* It sounded to me like the dumbest idea. Don't get me wrong, I love poetry. I'd read plenty of the greats as part of my degree — from Emily Dickenson to Langston Hughes — but I didn't think of myself as a poet. A writer, yes. A poet, no. But my friend persisted.

I remember sitting at the dinning table watching our black Angora cat, Smokey, blithely hop onto the couch for a nap, and the low hiss of a space heater faintly in my ear. I remember reflecting on my day-to-day, on how I'd abruptly quit my job and found myself adrift, waking each morning riddled with dread, knowing that my husband would go off to work, my kids off to school, and I would be left home alone, surfing the web for jobs, and envying the cat her insouciant life. I gave my friend's suggestion serious thought. Why throw away months of hope and hard work? I decided to give it a try. At the very least it would give me something to do while I looked for work.

I wrote six terrible poems in a week. They were so bad I gave up in a fit of disgust. But then one night I had a dream in which my late maternal grandmother, Lilian, spoke the following words to me in her native Haitian Creole: *"Map grimpe ak cheveu'm, map grimpe!"* which roughly translates to, "I climb with my hair, I climb!" Needless to say, I took this as a sign. After the dream — and after learning from my mother that Lilian had been taught the Walker method by her mother, who had likely been trained by Walker agents, and that both women had been able to provide for their children as hair dressers — I dove back into the poetry. It wasn't long before I found my *flow*.

As it happened, writing this epic woman's story in verse became my sun of York, so to speak. Turning my winter of discontent into a glorious spring. Such was the joy it gave me. Instead of hiding under a blanket of despair and self-pity, as I had done for nearly three months, I began to wake each morning excited to get out of bed and get to work. As I got further along in the writing, I felt as if Madam C.J. Walker herself was visiting me, encouraging me along, my kind and generous muse. She lifted me out of my sunken place, as she had done for legions of black women before me, including my grandmother, whose dreamy missive became part of a haiku.

That I've re-told Walker's story through poetry is one of the things that I hope gives this book some relevance during these uncertain times. With the coronavirus pandemic upending daily life (so much for plans), and forcing us to shut down and face a tumultuous road ahead, poetry can be like a salve that invites a certain stillness into the fray, soaking the mind with its wonder and intensity, even if only for a few lines of verse. That's certainly true for good poetry. Did I write at least one good poem? I hope so.

To that end, I humbly acknowledge that this collection may not appeal to everyone, indeed it may appeal to no one. But for me it truly was like the sun breaking through a storm cloud.   I offer this work in honour of that gift.

R.A.

20 March 2020

ACKNOWLEDGMENTS

As always, I am grateful to all those who helped in the writing of this collection. Special thanks go to Janet Donald and Jane Hyde for your patient reading and diligent critiques, and to Craig Pearce for your encouragement and support. I am also grateful to A'Lelia Bundles, whose biographies on Madam Walker were the inspiration for this work.

Thanks and love to my family and friends. Particular thanks to Greta Lestage and Sidney Augustin. Very special thanks to Ben Keating, you're a legend. And to Angela Dawson, Samatha Morley, Dominic Johnson, and their brood, the most delightful bunch of people to grace the earth. Also my deepest gratitude to Patrik Henry Bass for your faith and the fabulous lunches. My most heartfelt thanks to my daughters, Marley and Stevie, who grow ever more enchanting and fierce with each passing day. You both rock. And, saving the very best for last, a million loving thanks to Tom, my R.O.D. What a *journey* we have had together. This is for you, with love.

ABOUT THE AUTHOR

Rojé Augustin is a native New Yorker who grew up on the Upper West Side of Manhattan. Her first novel, *The Unraveling of Bebe Jones*, won the 2013 National Indie Excellence Award in African American fiction. She wrote the novel while living in London and Sydney as a stay-at-home-mom. Rojé continues to work as a producer while also writing in her spare time. She lives in Sydney with her husband and two daughters.

www.ingramcontent.com/pod-product-compliance
Lightning Source LLC
Chambersburg PA
CBHW031252060726
47590CB00003B/878